BEST LOVE POEMS
OF ALL TIME

GW01186478

CLASSICS

Reprint 2023

FiNGERPRINT! **CLASSICS**
An imprint of Prakash Books India Pvt. Ltd.

113/A, Darya Ganj,
New Delhi-110 002
Tel: (011) 2324 7062 – 65, Fax: (011) 2324 6975
Email: info@prakashbooks.com/sales@prakashbooks.com

facebook www.facebook.com/fingerprintpublishing
twitter www.twitter.com/FingerprintP
www.fingerprintpublishing.com

Selection and editorial material © Fingerprint! Publishing

ISBN: 978 93 8993 101 3

Processed & printed in India

The human mind often ponders the question—what is love?

When does it all start? Is it that magical moment, when the lovers see each other for the first time? And when does it all end, if at all? Till death does them part . . . or not even then?

Love . . . Words may never be enough to express it. It may be pure or fatal, fleeting or eternal, platonic or erotic, or may not fit into any categories at all. It is a feeling that is considered seemingly indescribable. Even so, poets over the years have attempted to describe it in their verse.

Each poet has, at some point in their lives, fallen in love and then written about it. It is like *a red rose freshly sprung in June* for Robert Burns, an emotion that *never alters when it alteration finds* for William Shakespeare, and something that troubles young hearts for Thomas Wyatt.

Inarguably, the most famous lines written on love have been by William Shakespeare. His love sonnets, published four hundred years ago, are widely read and quoted even today. The sonnets capture the sincere emotions of a lover, who delivers panegyrics on his beloved's beauty. The intimate feelings conveyed in the sonnets almost make the readers feel like intruders, overhearing the lover's private, almost embarrassing thoughts. Though this sense of eavesdropping exists in almost all the love poems written.

Porphyria's lover in Robert Browning's poem of the same name does not know that the reader has seen him strangle his beloved. As the lover justifies his act, the readers chastise him for being jealous and possessive. The poet-lover in Edward Thomas' poem does not know that as he waits for his beloved to come and meet him, the reader is waiting with him.

From the love poems written by Alfred Tennyson to those by William Wordsworth, this compilation of poems spans from the powerful sixteenth century love poetry, when lovers longed for their beautiful, unattainable beloveds, to the simple, yet elegant, twentieth century love poetry.

Watch as the lovers fall for each other, make promises of undying love, suffer heartbreaks, deceive, grow bitter, jealous, and even obsessed and disastrously possessive. Some poems in this edition are short and sweet, others are long and beautiful, some rhyme, others don't . . . and all of them are about love.

Contents

Mariana

by Alfred Tennyson

With blackest moss the flower-plots
Were thickly crusted, one and all:
The rusted nails fell from the knots
That held the pear to the gable-wall.
The broken sheds look'd sad and strange:
Unlifted was the clinking latch;
Weeded and worn the ancient thatch
Upon the lonely moated grange.
She only said, "My life is dreary,
He cometh not," she said;
She said, "I am aweary, aweary,
I would that I were dead!"

Her tears fell with the dews at even;
Her tears fell ere the dews were dried;

She could not look on the sweet heaven,
Either at morn or eventide.
After the flitting of the bats,
When thickest dark did trance the sky,
She drew her casement-curtain by,
And glanced athwart the glooming flats.
She only said, "The night is dreary,
He cometh not," she said;
She said, "I am aweary, aweary,
I would that I were dead!"

Upon the middle of the night,
Waking she heard the night-fowl crow:
The cock sung out an hour ere light:
From the dark fen the oxen's low
Came to her: without hope of change,
In sleep she seem'd to walk forlorn,
Till cold winds woke the gray-eyed morn
About the lonely moated grange.
She only said, "The day is dreary,
He cometh not," she said;
She said, "I am aweary, aweary,
I would that I were dead!"

About a stone-cast from the wall
A sluice with blacken'd waters slept,
And o'er it many, round and small,

The cluster'd marish-mosses crept.
Hard by a poplar shook alway,
All silver-green with gnarled bark:
For leagues no other tree did mark
The level waste, the rounding gray.
She only said, "My life is dreary,
He cometh not," she said;
She said "I am aweary, aweary
I would that I were dead!"

And ever when the moon was low,
And the shrill winds were up and away,
In the white curtain, to and fro,
She saw the gusty shadow sway.
But when the moon was very low
And wild winds bound within their cell,
The shadow of the poplar fell
Upon her bed, across her brow.
She only said, "The night is dreary,
He cometh not," she said;
She said "I am aweary, aweary,
I would that I were dead!"

All day within the dreamy house,
The doors upon their hinges creak'd;
The blue fly sung in the pane; the mouse
Behind the mouldering wainscot shriek'd,

Or from the crevice peer'd about.
Old faces glimmer'd thro' the doors
Old footsteps trod the upper floors,
Old voices called her from without.
She only said, "My life is dreary,
He cometh not," she said;
She said, "I am aweary, aweary,
I would that I were dead!"

The sparrow's chirrup on the roof,
The slow clock ticking, and the sound
Which to the wooing wind aloof
The poplar made, did all confound
Her sense; but most she loathed the hour
When the thick-moted sunbeam lay
Athwart the chambers, and the day
Was sloping toward his western bower.
Then said she, "I am very dreary,
He will not come," she said;
She wept, "I am aweary, aweary,
Oh God, that I were dead!"

Marriage Morning

by Alfred Tennyson

Light, so low upon earth,
    You send a flash to the sun.
    Here is the golden close of love,
    All my wooing is done.
    Oh, the woods and the meadows,
    Woods where we hid from the wet,
    Stiles where we stay'd to be kind,
    Meadows in which we met!

    Light, so low in the vale
    You flash and lighten afar,
    For this is the golden morning of love,
    And you are his morning start.
    Flash, I am coming, I come,
    By meadow and stile and wood,

Oh, lighten into my eyes and heart,
Into my heart and my blood!

Heart, are you great enough
For a love that never tires?
O' heart, are you great enough for love?
I have heard of thorns and briers,
Over the meadow and stiles,
Over the world to the end of it
Flash for a million miles.

Not at All, or All in All

by Alfred Tennyson

In Love, if Love be Love, if Love be ours,
Faith and unfaith can ne'er be equal powers;
Unfaith in aught is want of faith in all.

It is the little rift within the lute,
That by and by will make the music mute,
And ever widening slowly silence all.

The little rift within the lover's lute
Or little pitted speck in garnered fruit,
That rotting inward, slowly molders all.

It is not worth the keeping: let it go:
But shall it? answer, darling, answer, no.
And trust me not at all or all in all.

The Lady of Shalott

by Alfred Tennyson

PART I

On either side the river lie
Long fields of barley and of rye,
That clothe the wold and meet the sky;
And thro' the field the road runs by
    To many-tower'd Camelot;
And up and down the people go,
Gazing where the lilies blow
Round an island there below,
    The island of Shalott.

Willows whiten, aspens quiver,
Little breezes dusk and shiver
Thro' the wave that runs for ever

By the island in the river
    Flowing down to Camelot.
Four gray walls, and four gray towers,
Overlook a space of flowers,
And the silent isle imbowers
    The Lady of Shalott.

By the margin, willow-veil'd,
Slide the heavy barges trail'd
By slow horses; and unhail'd
The shallop flitteth silken-sail'd
    Skimming down to Camelot:
But who hath seen her wave her hand?
Or at the casement seen her stand?
Or is she known in all the land,
    The Lady of Shalott?

Only reapers, reaping early
In among the bearded barley,
Hear a song that echoes cheerly
From the river winding clearly,
    Down to tower'd Camelot:
And by the moon the reaper weary,
Piling sheaves in uplands airy,
Listening, whispers ''Tis the fairy
    Lady of Shalott.'

PART II

There she weaves by night and day
A magic web with colours gay.
She has heard a whisper say,
A curse is on her if she stay
    To look down to Camelot.
She knows not what the curse may be,
And so she weaveth steadily,
And little other care hath she,
    The Lady of Shalott.

And moving thro' a mirror clear
That hangs before her all the year,
Shadows of the world appear.
There she sees the highway near
    Winding down to Camelot:
There the river eddy whirls,
And there the surly village-churls,
And the red cloaks of market girls,
    Pass onward from Shalott.

Sometimes a troop of damsels glad,
An abbot on an ambling pad,
Sometimes a curly shepherd-lad,
Or long-hair'd page in crimson clad,
    Goes by to tower'd Camelot;

And sometimes thro' the mirror blue
The knights come riding two and two:
She hath no loyal knight and true,
    The Lady of Shalott.

But in her web she still delights
To weave the mirror's magic sights,
For often thro' the silent nights
A funeral, with plumes and lights,
    And music, went to Camelot:
Or when the moon was overhead,
Came two young lovers lately wed;
'I am half sick of shadows,' said
    The Lady of Shalott.

PART III

A bow-shot from her bower-eaves,
He rode between the barley-sheaves,
The sun came dazzling thro' the leaves,
And flamed upon the brazen greaves
    Of bold Sir Lancelot.
A red-cross knight for ever kneel'd
To a lady in his shield,
That sparkled on the yellow field,
    Beside remote Shalott.

The gemmy bridle glitter'd free,
Like to some branch of stars we see
Hung in the golden Galaxy.
The bridle bells rang merrily
    As he rode down to Camelot:
And from his blazon'd baldric slung
A mighty silver bugle hung,
And as he rode his armour rung,
    Beside remote Shalott.

All in the blue unclouded weather
Thick-jewell'd shone the saddle-leather,
The helmet and the helmet-feather
Burn'd like one burning flame together,
As he rode down to Camelot.
    As often thro' the purple night,
Below the starry clusters bright,
Some bearded meteor, trailing light,
    Moves over still Shalott.

His broad clear brow in sunlight glow'd;
On burnish'd hooves his war-horse trode;
From underneath his helmet flow'd
His coal-black curls as on he rode,
    As he rode down to Camelot.
From the bank and from the river
He flash'd into the crystal mirror,

'Tirra lirra,' by the river
    Sang Sir Lancelot.

She left the web, she left the loom,
She made three paces thro' the room,
She saw the water-lily bloom,
She saw the helmet and the plume,
    She look'd down to Camelot.
Out flew the web and floated wide;
The mirror crack'd from side to side;
'The curse is come upon me!' cried
    The Lady of Shalott.

PART IV

In the stormy east-wind straining,
The pale yellow woods were waning,
The broad stream in his banks complaining,
Heavily the low sky raining
    Over tower'd Camelot;

Down she came and found a boat
Beneath a willow left afloat,
And round about the prow she wrote
    The Lady of Shalott.

And down the river's dim expanse—
Like some bold seer in a trance,
Seeing all his own mischance—
With a glassy countenance
    Did she look to Camelot.
And at the closing of the day
She loosed the chain, and down she lay;
The broad stream bore her far away,
      The Lady of Shalott.

Lying, robed in snowy white
That loosely flew to left and right—
The leaves upon her falling light—
Thro' the noises of the night
    She floated down to Camelot:
And as the boat-head wound along
The willowy hills and fields among,
They heard her singing her last song,
      The Lady of Shalott.

Heard a carol, mournful, holy,
Chanted loudly, chanted lowly,
Till her blood was frozen slowly,
And her eyes were darken'd wholly,
    Turn'd to tower'd Camelot;
For ere she reach'd upon the tide
The first house by the water-side,

Singing in her song she died,
    The Lady of Shalott.

Under tower and balcony,
By garden-wall and gallery,
A gleaming shape she floated by,
Dead-pale between the houses high,
    Silent into Camelot.
Out upon the wharfs they came,
Knight and burgher, lord and dame,
And round the prow they read her name,
    The Lady of Shalott.

Who is this? and what is here?
And in the lighted palace near
Died the sound of royal cheer;
And they cross'd themselves for fear,
    All the knights at Camelot:
But Lancelot mused a little space;
He said, 'She has a lovely face;
God in His mercy lend her grace,
    The Lady of Shalott.'

The Definition of Love

by Andrew Marvell

My love is of a birth as rare
As 'tis for object strange and high;
It was begotten by Despair
Upon Impossibility.

Magnanimous Despair alone
Could show me so divine a thing
Where feeble Hope could ne'er have flown,
But vainly flapp'd its tinsel wing.

And yet I quickly might arrive
Where my extended soul is fixt,
But Fate does iron wedges drive,
And always crowds itself betwixt.

For Fate with jealous eye does see
Two perfect loves, nor lets them close;
Their union would her ruin be,
And her tyrannic pow'r depose.

And therefore her decrees of steel
Us as the distant poles have plac'd,
(Though love's whole world on us doth wheel)
Not by themselves to be embrac'd;

Unless the giddy heaven fall,
And earth some new convulsion tear;
And, us to join, the world should all
Be cramp'd into a planisphere.

As lines, so loves oblique may well
Themselves in every angle greet;
But ours so truly parallel,
Though infinite, can never meet.

Therefore the love which us doth bind,
But Fate so enviously debars,
Is the conjunction of the mind,
And opposition of the stars.

To His Coy Mistress

by Andrew Marvell

Had we but world enough and time,
This coyness, lady, were no crime.
We would sit down, and think which way
To walk, and pass our long love's day.
Thou by the Indian Ganges' side
Shouldst rubies find; I by the tide
Of Humber would complain. I would
Love you ten years before the flood,
And you should, if you please, refuse
Till the conversion of the Jews.
My vegetable love should grow
Vaster than empires and more slow;
An hundred years should go to praise
Thine eyes, and on thy forehead gaze;
Two hundred to adore each breast,

But thirty thousand to the rest;
An age at least to every part,
And the last age should show your heart.
For, lady, you deserve this state,
Nor would I love at lower rate.

But at my back I always hear
Time's wingèd chariot hurrying near;
And yonder all before us lie
Deserts of vast eternity.
Thy beauty shall no more be found;
Nor, in thy marble vault, shall sound
My echoing song; then worms shall try
That long-preserved virginity,
And your quaint honour turn to dust,
And into ashes all my lust;
The grave's a fine and private place,
But none, I think, do there embrace.

Now therefore, while the youthful hue
Sits on thy skin like morning dew,
And while thy willing soul transpires
At every pore with instant fires,
Now let us sport us while we may,
And now, like amorous birds of prey,
Rather at once our time devour
Than languish in his slow-chapped power.

Let us roll all our strength and all
Our sweetness up into one ball,
And tear our pleasures with rough strife
Through the iron gates of life:
Thus, though we cannot make our sun
Stand still, yet we will make him run.

Love Me Little,
Love Me Long

by Anonymous

Love me little, love me long!
Is the burden of my song:
Love that is too hot and strong
    Burneth soon to waste.
Still I would not have thee cold,—
Not too backward, nor too bold;
Love that lasteth till 't is old
    Fadeth not in haste.
Love me little, love me long!
Is the burden of my song.

If thou lovest me too much,
'T will not prove as true a touch;
Love me little more than such,—
    For I fear the end.

I 'm with little well content,
And a little from thee sent
Is enough, with true intent
    To be steadfast, friend.

Say thou lovest me, while thou live
I to thee my love will give,
Never dreaming to deceive
    While that life endures;
Nay, and after death, in sooth,
I to thee will keep my truth,
As now when in my May of youth:
    This my love assures.

Constant love is moderate ever,
And it will through life persever;
Give me that with true endeavor,—
    I will it restore.
A suit of durance let it be,
For all weathers,—that for me,—
For the land or for the sea:
    Lasting evermore.

Winter's cold or summer's heat,
Autumn's tempests on it beat;
It can never know defeat,
    Never can rebel.

Such the love that I would gain,
Such the love, I tell thee plain,
Thou must give, or woo in vain:
    So to thee—farewell!

The Faithful Lovers

by Anonymous

I'd been away from her three years,—about
    that,
    And I returned to find my Mary true;
And though I 'd question her, I did not doubt
    that
    It was unnecessary so to do.

'T was by the chimney-corner we were sitting:
    "Mary," said I, "have you been always true?"
"Frankly," says she, just pausing in her knitting,
    "I don't think I 've unfaithful been to you:
But for the three years past I 'll tell you what
I 've done; then say if I 've been true or not.

"When first you left my grief was uncontrollable;
  Alone I mourned my miserable lot;
And all who saw me thought me inconsolable,
  Till Captain Clifford came from Aldershot.
To flirt with him amused me while 't was new:
I don't count that unfaithfulness—do you?

"The next—oh! let me see—was Frankie Phipps;
  I met him at my uncle's, Christmas-tide,
And 'neath the mistletoe, where lips meet lips,
  He gave me his first kiss—" And here she sighed.
"We stayed six weeks at uncle's—how time flew!
I don't count that unfaithfulness—do you?

"Lord Cecil Fossmore—only twenty-one—
  Lent me his horse. O, how we rode and raced!
We scoured the downs—we rode to hounds—such
    fun!
  And often was his arm about my waist,—
That was to lift me up and down. But who
Would call just that unfaithfulness? Would you?

"Do you know Reggy Vere? Ah, how he sings!
  We met,—'t was at a picnic. O such weather!
He gave me, look, the first of these two rings
  When we were lost in Cliefden woods together.

Ah, what a happy time we spent,—we two!
I don't count that unfaithfulness to you.

"I 've yet another ring from him; d'ye see
    The plain gold circlet that is shining here?"
I took her hand: "O Mary! can it be
    That you—" Quoth she, "that I am Mrs. Vere.
I don't call that unfaithfulness—do you?"
"No," I replied, "for I am married too."

Song

by Aphra Behn

O Love! that stronger art than wine,
Pleasing delusion, witchery divine,
Wont to be prized above all wealth,
Disease that has more joys than health;
Though we blaspheme thee in our pain,
And of thy tyranny complain,
We are all bettered by they reign.

What reason never can bestow
We to this useful passion owe;
Love wakes the dull from sluggish ease,
And learns a clown the art to please,
Humbles the vain, kindles the cold,
Makes misers free, and cowards bold;

'Tis he reforms the sot from drink,
And teaches airy fops to think.

When full brute appetite is fed,
And choked the glutton lies and dead,
Thou new spirits dost dispense
And 'finest the gross delights of sense:
Virtue's unconquerable aid
That against Nature can persuade,
And makes a roving mind retire
Within the bounds of just desire;
Cheerer of age, youth's kind unrest,
And half the heaven of the blest!

To Celia

by Ben Jonson

Drink to me only with thine eyes,
  And I will pledge with mine;
Or leave a kiss but in the cup,
  And I 'll not look for wine.
The thirst that from the soul doth rise
  Doth ask a drink divine;
But might I of Jove's nectar sup,
  I would not change for thine.

I sent thee late a rosy wreath,
  Not so much honoring thee
As giving it a hope that there
  It could not withered be;
But thou thereon didst only breathe

And sent'st it back to me;
Since when it grows, and smells, I swear,
      Not of itself but thee!

Not Ours the Vows

by Bernard Barton

Not ours the vows of such as plight
    Their troth in sunny weather,
While leaves are green and skies are bright,
    To walk on flowers together.

But we have loved as those who tread
    The thorny path of sorrow,
With clouds above, and cause to dread
    Yet deeper gloom to-morrow.

That thorny path, those stormy skies,
    Have drawn our spirits nearer;
And rendered us, by sorrow's ties,
    Each to the other dearer.

Love, born in hours of joy and mirth,
　　With mirth and joy may perish;
That to which darker hours gave birth
　　Still more and more we cherish.

It looks beyond the clouds of time,
　　And through death's shadowy portal;
Made by adversity sublime,
　　By faith and hope immortal.

I Do Not Love Thee

by Caroline Elizabeth Sarah Norton

I do not love thee!—no! I do not love thee!
And yet when thou art absent I am sad;
   And envy even the bright blue sky above
      thee,
Whose quiet stars may see thee and be glad.

I do not love thee!—yet, I know not why,
Whate'er thou dost seems still well done, to me:
   And often in my solitude I sigh
That those I do love are not more like thee!

I do not love thee!—yet, when thou art
      gone,
I hate the sound (though those who speak be
     dear)

Which breaks the lingering echo of the tone
Thy voice of music leaves upon my ear.

I do not love thee!—yet thy speaking eyes,
With their deep, bright, and most expressive blue,
Between me and the midnight heaven arise,
Oftener than any eyes I ever knew.

I know I do not love thee! yet, alas!
Others will scarcely trust my candid heart;
And oft I catch them smiling as they pass,
Because they see me gazing where thou art.

The Fire of Love

by Charles Sackville

The fire of love in youthful blood,
Like what is kindled in brushwood,
 But for a moment burns;
Yet in that moment makes a mighty noise;
It crackles, and to vapor turns,
 And soon itself destroys.

But when crept into agèd veins
It slowly burns, and then long remains,
 And with a silent heat,
Like fire in logs, it glows and warms 'em long,
And though the name be not so great,
 Yet is the heat as strong.

After Death

by Christina Rossetti

The curtains were half drawn, the floor was
    swept
And strewn with rushes, rosemary and may
Lay thick upon the bed on which I lay,
Where through the lattice ivy-shadows crept.
He leaned above me, thinking that I slept
And could not hear him; but I heard him say,
'Poor child, poor child': and as he turned away
Came a deep silence, and I knew he wept.
He did not touch the shroud, or raise the fold
That hid my face, or take my hand in his,
Or ruffle the smooth pillows for my head:
He did not love me living; but once dead
He pitied me; and very sweet it is
To know he still is warm though I am cold.

Maiden-Song

by Christina Rossetti

Long ago and long ago,
    And long ago still,
There dwelt three merry maidens
    Upon a distant hill.
One was tall Meggan,
    And one was dainty May,
But one was fair Margaret,
    More fair than I can say,
Long ago and long ago.

When Meggan plucked the thorny rose,
    And when May pulled the brier,
Half the birds would swoop to see,
    Half the beasts draw nigher;
Half the fishes of the streams

Would dart up to admire:
But when Margaret plucked a flag-flower,
    Or poppy hot aflame,
All the beasts and all the birds
    And all the fishes came
To her hand more soft than snow.

Strawberry leaves and May-dew
    In brisk morning air,
Strawberry leaves and May-dew
    Make maidens fair.
"I go for strawberry-leaves,"
    Meggan said one day:
"Fair Margaret can bide at home,
    But you come with me, May;
Up the hill and down the hill,
    Along the winding way,
You and I are used to go."

So these two fair sisters
    Went with innocent will
Up the hill and down again,
    And round the homestead hill:
While the fairest sat at home,
    Margaret like a queen,
Like a blush-rose, like the moon
    In her heavenly sheen,

Fragrant-breathed as milky cow
    Or field of blossoming bean,
Graceful as an ivy bough
    Born to cling and lean;
Thus she sat to sing and sew.

When she raised her lustrous eyes
    A beast peeped at the door;
When she downward cast her eyes
    A fish gasped on the floor;
When she turned away her eyes
    A bird perched on the sill,
Warbling out its heart of love,
    Warbling, warbling still,
With pathetic pleadings low.

Light-foot May with Meggan
    Sought the choicest spot,
Clothed with thyme-alternate grass:
    Then, while day waxed hot,
Sat at ease to play and rest,
    A gracious rest and play;
The loveliest maidens near or far,
    When Margaret was away,
Who sat at home to sing and sew.

Sun-glow flushed their comely cheeks,

Wind-play tossed their hair,
Creeping things among the grass
    Stroked them here and there;
Meggan piped a merry note,
    A fitful, wayward lay,
While shrill as bird on topmost twig
    Piped merry May;
Honey-smooth the double flow.

Sped a herdsman from the vale,
    Mounting like a flame,
All on fire to hear and see
    With floating locks he came.
Looked neither north nor south,
    Neither east nor west,
But sat him down at Meggan's feet
    As love-bird on his nest,
And wooed her with a silent awe,
    With trouble not expressed;
She sang the tears into his eyes,
    The heart out of his breast:
So he loved her, listening so.

She sang the heart out of his breast,
    The words out of his tongue;
Hand and foot and pulse he paused
    Till her song was sung.

Then he spoke up from his place
    Simple words and true:
"Scanty goods have I to give,
    Scanty skill to woo;
But I have a will to work,
    And a heart for you:
Bid me stay or bid me go."

Then Meggan mused within herself:
    "Better be first with him,
Than dwell where fairer Margaret sits,
    Who shines my brightness dim,
Forever second where she sits,
    However fair I be:
I will be lady of his love,
    And he shall worship me;
I will be lady of his herds
    And stoop to his degree,
At home where kids and fatlings grow."

Sped a shepherd from the height
    Headlong down to look,
(White lambs followed, lured by love
    Of their shepherd's crook):
He turned neither east nor west,
    Neither north nor south,
But knelt right down to May, for love

Of her sweet-singing mouth;
Forgot his flocks, his panting flocks
    In parching hillside drouth;
Forgot himself for weal or woe.

Trilled her song and swelled her song
    With maiden coy caprice
In a labyrinth of throbs,
    Pauses, cadences;
Clear-noted as a dropping brook,
    Soft-noted like the bees,
Wild-noted as the shivering wind
    Forlorn through forest trees:
Love-noted like the wood-pigeon
    Who hides herself for love,
Yet cannot keep her secret safe,
    But cooes and cooes thereof:
Thus the notes rang loud or low.

He hung breathless on her breath;
    Speechless, who listened well;
Could not speak or think or wish
    Till silence broke the spell.
Then he spoke, and spread his hands
    Pointing here and there:
"See my sheep and see the lambs,
    Twin lambs which they bare.

All myself I offer you,
    All my flocks and care,
Your sweet song hath moved me so."

In her fluttered heart young May
    Mused a dubious while:
"If he loves me as he says"—
    Her lips curved with a smile:
"Where Margaret shines like the sun,
    I shine but like a moon;
If sister Meggan makes her choice
    I can make mine as soon;
At cockcrow we were sister-maids,
    We may be brides at noon."
Said Meggan, "Yes"; May said not "No."

Fair Margaret stayed alone at home,
    Awhile she sang her song,
Awhile sat silent, then she thought:
    "My sisters loiter long."
That sultry noon had waned away,
    Shadows had waxen great:
"Surely," she thought within herself,
    "My sisters loiter late."
She rose, and peered out at the door,
    With patient heart to wait,
And heard a distant nightingale

Complaining of its mate;
Then down the garden slope she walked,
    Down to the garden gate,
Leaned on the rail and waited so.

The slope was lightened by her eyes
    Like summer lightning fair,
Like rising of the haloed moon
    Lightened her glimmering hair,
While her face lightened like the sun
    Whose dawn is rosy white.
Thus crowned with maiden majesty
    She peered into the night,
Looked up the hill and down the hill,
    To left hand and to right,
Flashing like fire-flies to and fro.

Waiting thus in weariness
    She marked the nightingale
Telling, if any one would heed,
    Its old complaining tale.
Then lifted she her voice and sang,
    Answering the bird:
Then lifted she her voice and sang,
    Such notes were never heard
From any bird when Spring's in blow.

The king of all that country
    Coursing far, coursing near,
Curbed his amber-bitted steed,
    Coursed amain to hear;
All his princes in his train,
    Squire, and knight, and peer,
With his crown upon his head,
    His sceptre in his hand,
Down he fell at Margaret's knees
    Lord king of all that land,
To her highness bending low.

Every beast and bird and fish
    Came mustering to the sound,
Every man and every maid
    From miles of country round:
Meggan on her herdsman's arm,
    With her shepherd, May,
Flocks and herds trooped at their heels
    Along the hillside way;
No foot too feeble for the ascent,
    Not any head too gray;
Some were swift and none were slow.

So Margaret sang her sisters home
    In their marriage mirth;
Sang free birds out of the sky,

Beasts along the earth,
Sang up fishes of the deep,—
  All breathing things that move
Sang from far and sang from near
  To her lovely love;
Sang together friend and foe;

Sang a golden-bearded king
  Straightway to her feet,
Sang him silent where he knelt
  In eager anguish sweet.
But when the clear voice died away,
  When longest echoes died,
He stood up like a royal man
  And claimed her for his bride.
So three maids were wooed and won
  In a brief May-tide,
Long ago and long ago.

Dream-Love

by Christina Rossetti

Young Love lies sleeping
In May-time of the year,
Among the lilies,
Lapped in the tender light:
White lambs come grazing,
White doves come building there:
And round about him
The May-bushes are white.

Soft moss the pillow
For oh, a softer cheek;
Broad leaves cast shadow
Upon the heavy eyes:
There winds and waters

Grow lulled and scarcely speak;
There twilight lingers
The longest in the skies.

Young Love lies dreaming;
But who shall tell the dream?
A perfect sunlight
On rustling forest tips;
Or perfect moonlight
Upon a rippling stream;
Or perfect silence,
Or song of cherished lips.

Burn odours round him
To fill the drowsy air;
Weave silent dances
Around him to and fro;
For oh, in waking
The sights are not so fair,
And song and silence
Are not like these below.

Young Love lies dreaming
Till summer days are gone,—
Dreaming and drowsing
Away to perfect sleep:

He sees the beauty
Sun hath not looked upon,
And tastes the fountain
Unutterably deep.

Him perfect music
Doth hush unto his rest,
And through the pauses
The perfect silence calms:
Oh, poor the voices
Of earth from east to west,
And poor earth's stillness
Between her stately palms.

Young Love lies drowsing
Away to poppied death;
Cool shadows deepen
Across the sleeping face:
So fails the summer
With warm, delicious breath;
And what hath autumn
To give us in its place?

Draw close the curtains
Of branched evergreen;
Change cannot touch them

With fading fingers sere:
Here the first violets
Perhaps will bud unseen,
And a dove, may be,
Return to nestle here.

I Loved You First

by Christina Rossetti

I loved you first: but afterwards your love
Outsoaring mine, sang such a loftier song
As drowned the friendly cooings of my dove.
Which owes the other most? my love was long,
And yours one moment seemed to wax more
    strong;
I loved and guessed at you, you construed me
And loved me for what might or might not be—
Nay, weights and measures do us both a
    wrong.
For verily love knows not 'mine' or 'thine;'
With separate 'I' and 'thou' free love has done,
For one is both and both are one in love:

Rich love knows nought of 'thine that is not mine;'
Both have the strength and both the length
    thereof,
Both of us, of the love which makes us one.

I Wish I Could Remember

by Christina Rossetti

I wish I could remember that first day,
First hour, first moment of your meeting me,
If bright or dim the season, it might be
Summer or Winter for aught I can say;
So unrecorded did it slip away,
So blind was I to see and to foresee,
So dull to mark the budding of my tree
That would not blossom yet for many a May.
If only I could recollect it, such
A day of days! I let it come and go
As traceless as a thaw of bygone snow;
It seemed to mean so little, meant so much;
If only now I could recall that touch,
First touch of hand in hand—Did one but
    know!

When I Am Dead

by Christina Rossetti

When I am dead, my dearest,
    Sing no sad songs for me;
Plant thou no roses at my head,
    Nor shady cypress tree:
Be the green grass above me
    With showers and dewdrops wet:
And if thou wilt, remember,
    And if thou wilt, forget.

I shall not see the shadows,
    I shall not feel the rain;
I shall not hear the nightingale
    Sing on as if in pain:

And dreaming through the twilight
    That doth not rise nor set,
Haply I may remember,
    And haply may forget.

The Passionate Shepherd to His Love

by Christopher Marlowe

Come live with me and be my love,
And we will all the pleasures prove,
That Valleys, groves, hills, and fields,
Woods, or steepy mountain yields.

And we will sit upon the Rocks,
Seeing the Shepherds feed their flocks,
By shallow Rivers to whose falls
Melodious birds sing Madrigals.

And I will make thee beds of Roses
And a thousand fragrant posies,
A cap of flowers, and a kirtle
Embroidered all with leaves of Myrtle;

A gown made of the finest wool
Which from our pretty Lambs we pull;
Fair lined slippers for the cold,
With buckles of the purest gold;

A belt of straw and Ivy buds,
With Coral clasps and Amber studs:
And if these pleasures may thee move,
Come live with me, and be my love.

The Shepherds' Swains shall dance and sing
For thy delight each May-morning:
If these delights thy mind may move,
Then live with me, and be my love.

My Lady

by Dante Alighieri

My lady looks so gentle and so pure
    When yielding salutation by the way,
    That the tongue trembles and has nought
        to say,
And the eyes, which fain would see, may not
    endure.
And still, amid the praise she hears secure,
    She walks with humbleness for her array;
    Seeming a creature sent from Heaven to
        stay
On earth, and show a miracle made sure.
She is so pleasant in the eyes of men
That through the sight the inmost heart doth
    gain

A sweetness which needs proof to know it by:
And from between her lips there seems to move
A soothing essence that is full of love,
Saying for ever to the spirit, "Sigh!"

Gloire de Dijon

by D H Lawrence

When she rises in the morning
I linger to watch her;
She spreads the bath-cloth underneath the
    window
And the sunbeams catch her
Glistening white on the shoulders,
While down her sides the mellow
Golden shadow glows as
She stoops to the sponge, and her swung breasts
Sway like full-blown yellow
Gloire de Dijon roses.

She drips herself with water, and her shoulders
Glisten as silver, they crumple up
Like wet and falling roses, and I listen

For the sluicing of their rain-dishevelled petals.
In the window full of sunlight
Concentrates her golden shadow
Fold on fold, until it glows as
Mellow as the glory roses.

Annabel Lee

by Edgar Allan Poe

It was many and many a year ago,
    In a kingdom by the sea,
That a maiden there lived whom you may know
    By the name of Annabel Lee;
And this maiden she lived with no other
    thought
    Than to love and be loved by me.

I was a child and *she* was a child,
    In this kingdom by the sea,
But we loved with a love that was more than
    love—
    I and my Annabel Lee;
With a love that the wingèd seraphs of heaven
    Coveted her and me.

And this was the reason that, long ago,
    In this kingdom by the sea,
A wind blew out of a cloud, chilling
    My beautiful Annabel Lee;
So that her highborn kinsman came
    And bore her away from me,
To shut her up in a sepulchre
    In this kingdom by the sea.

The angels, not half so happy in heaven,
    Went envying her and me—
Yes!—that was the reason (as all men know,
    In this kingdom by the sea)
That the wind came out of the cloud by night,
    Chilling and killing my Annabel Lee.

But our love it was stronger by far than the love
    Of those who were older than we—
    Of many far wiser than we—
And neither the angels in heaven above
    Nor the demons down under the sea
Can ever dissever my soul from the soul
    Of the beautiful Annabel Lee.

For the moon never beams, without bringing me
    dreams
    Of the beautiful Annabel Lee;

And the stars never rise, but I feel the bright eyes
    Of the beautiful Annabel Lee;
And so, all the night-tide, I lie down by the side
    Of my darling—my darling—my life and my
        bride,
     In her sepulchre there by the sea,
     In her tomb by the sounding sea.

To Helen

by Edgar Allan Poe

Helen, thy beauty is to me
    Like those Nicéan barks of yore,
That gently, o'er a perfumed sea,
    The weary, way-worn wanderer bore
    To his own native shore.

On desperate seas long wont to roam,
    Thy hyacinth hair, thy classic face,
Thy Naiad airs have brought me home
    To the glory that was Greece,
    And the grandeur that was Rome.

Lo! in yon brilliant window-niche
    How statue-like I see thee stand,

The agate lamp within thy hand!
  A Psyche from the regions which
  Are Holy-Land!

My Love is Like to Ice

by Edmund Spenser

My love is like to ice, and I to fire;
How comes it then that this her cold so great
Is not dissolv'd through my so hot desire,
But harder grows the more I her entreat?
Or how comes it that my exceeding heat
Is not delay'd by her heart-frozen cold;
But that I burn much more in boiling sweat,
And feel my flames augmented manifold!
What more miraculous thing may be told,
That fire, which all things melts, should harden
     ice;
And ice, which is congeal'd with senseless cold,
Should kindle fire by wonderful device!
     Such is the power of love in gentle mind,
     That it can alter all the course of kind.

Was It a Dream

by Edmund Spenser

Was it a dream, or did I see it plain;
A goodly table of pure ivory,
All spread with junkets, fit to entertain
The greatest Prince with pompous royalty:
'Mongst which, there in a silver dish did lie
Two golden apples of unvalued price;
Far passing those which Hercules came by,
Or those which Atalanta did entice;
Exceeding sweet, yet void of sinful vice;
That many sought, yet none could ever taste;
Sweet fruit of pleasure, brought from Paradise
By Love himself, and in his garden placed.
    Her breast that table was, so richly spread;
    My thoughts the guests, which would
        thereon have fed.

Amoretti LXXV

by Edmund Spenser

One day I wrote her name upon the strand,
But came the waves and washed it away:
Again I wrote it with a second hand,
But came the tide, and made my pains his prey.
"Vain man," said she, "that dost in vain assay,
A mortal thing so to immortalize;
For I myself shall like to this decay,
And eke my name be wiped out likewise."
"Not so," (quod I) "let baser things devise
To die in dust, but you shall live by fame:
My verse your vertues rare shall eternize,
And in the heavens write your glorious name:
Where whenas death shall all the world subdue,
Our love shall live, and later life renew."

Will You Come

by Edward Thomas

Will you come?
Will you come?
Will you ride
So late
At my side?
O, will you come?

Will you come?
Will you come
If the night
Has a moon,
Full and bright?
O, will you come?

Would you come?
Would you come
If the noon
Gave light,
Not the moon?
Beautiful, would you come?

Would you have come?
Would you have come
Without scorning,
Had it been
Still morning?
Beloved, would you have come?

If you come
Haste and come.
Owls have cried;
It grows dark
To ride.
Beloved, beautiful, come.

Love Song

by Ella Wheeler Wilcox

Once in the world's first prime,
    When nothing lived or stirred—
Nothing but new-born Time,
    Nor was there even a bird—
The Silence spoke to a Star;
    But I do not dare repeat
What it said to its love afar,
    It was too sweet, too sweet.

But there, in the fair world's youth,
    Ere sorrow had drawn breath,
When nothing was known but Truth,
    Nor was there even death,
The Star to Silence was wed,
    And the Sun was priest that day,

And they made their bridal-bed
    High in the Milky Way.

For the great white star had heard
    Her silent lover's speech;
It needed no passionate word
    To pledge them each to each.
Oh, lady fair and far,
    Hear, oh, hear and apply!
Thou, the beautiful Star—
    The voiceless Silence, I.

Time and Love

by Ella Wheeler Wilcox

Time flies. The swift hours hurry by
    And speed us on to untried ways;
New seasons ripen, perish, die,
    And yet love stays.
The old, old love—like sweet, at first,
    At last like bitter wine—
I know not if it blest or curst
    Thy life and mine.

Time flies. In vain our prayers, our tears!
    We cannot tempt him to delays;
Down to the past he bears the years,
    And yet love stays.
Through changing task and varying dream
    We hear the same refrain,

As one can hear a plaintive theme
    Run through each strain.

Time flies. He steals our pulsing youth;
    He robs us of our care-free days;
He takes away our trust and truth:
    And yet love stays.
O Time! take love! When love is vain,
    When all its best joys die—
When only its regrets remain—
    Let love, too, fly.

Love and Friendship

by Emily Brontë

Love is like the wild rose-briar,
Friendship like the holly-tree—
The holly is dark when the rose-briar blooms
But which will bloom most constantly?

The wild rose-briar is sweet in spring,
Its summer blossoms scent the air;
Yet wait till winter comes again
And who will call the wild-briar fair?

Then scorn the silly rose-wreath now
And deck thee with the holly's sheen,
That when December blights thy brow
He still may leave thy garland green.

That I Did
Always Love

by Emily Dickinson

That I did always love
I bring thee Proof
That till I loved
I never lived—Enough—

That I shall love alway—
I argue thee
That love is life—
And life hath Immortality—

This—dost thou doubt—Sweet—
Then have I
Nothing to show
But Calvary—

Heart, We Will Forget Him

by Emily Dickinson

Heart, we will forget him!
  You and I, to-night!
You may forget the warmth he gave,
  I will forget the light.

When you have done, pray tell me,
  That I my thoughts may dim;
Haste! lest while you're lagging,
  I may remember him!

Wild Nights

by Emily Dickinson

Wild nights! Wild nights!
Were I with thee,
Wild nights should be
Our luxury!

Futile the winds
To a heart in port,
Done with the compass,
Done with the chart.

Rowing in Eden!
Ah! the sea!
Might I but moor
To-night in thee!

How Do I Love Thee

by Elizabeth Barrett Browning

How do I love thee? Let me count the ways.
I love thee to the depth and breadth and height
My soul can reach, when feeling out of sight
For the ends of Being and ideal Grace.
I love thee to the level of everyday's
Most quiet need, by sun and candlelight.
I love thee freely, as men might strive for Right;
I love thee purely, as they turn from Praise.
I love thee with the passion put to use
In my old griefs, and with my childhood's faith.
I love thee with a love I seemed to lose
With my lost saints,—I love thee with the breath,
Smiles, tears, of all my life! And, if God choose,
I shall but love thee better after death.

If Thou Must Love Me

by Elizabeth Barrett Browning

If thou must love me, let it be for nought
Except for love's sake only. Do not say
"I love her for her smile—her look—her way
Of speaking gently,—for a trick of thought
That falls in well with mine, and certes brought
A sense of pleasant ease on such a day"—
For these things in themselves, Belovèd, may
Be changed, or change for thee,—and love, so
    wrought,
May be unwrought so. Neither love me for
Thine own dear pity's wiping my cheeks dry,—
A creature might forget to weep, who bore
Thy comfort long, and lose thy love thereby!
But love me for love's sake, that evermore
    Thou may'st love on, through love's eternity.

When Do I See Thee Most

by Dante Gabriel Rossetti

When do I see thee most, beloved one?
When in the light the spirits of mine eyes
Before thy face, their altar, solemnize
The worship of that Love through thee made known?
Or when, in the dusk hours (we two alone),
Close-kissed, and eloquent of still replies
Thy twilight-hidden glimmering visage lies,
And my soul only sees thy soul its own?
O love, my love! if I no more should see
Thyself, nor on the earth the shadow of thee,
Nor image of thine eyes in any spring,—
How then should sound upon Life's darkening slope
The ground-whirl of the perished leaves of Hope,
The wind of Death's imperishable wing!

To One That Asked Me Why I Loved J.G.

by Ephelia

Why do I love? go ask the glorious sun
Why every day it round the world doth run:
Ask Thames and Tiber why they ebb and flow:
Ask damask roses why in June they blow:
Ask ice and hail the reason why they're cold:
Decaying beauties, why they will grow old:
They'll tell thee, Fate, that everything doth
    move,
Inforces them to this, and me to love.
There is no reason for our love or hate,
'Tis irresistible as Death or Fate;
'Tis not his face; I've sense enough to see,
That is not good, though doated on by me:
Nor is't his tongue, that has this conquest won,
For that at least is equalled by my own:

His carriage can to none obliging be,
'Tis rude, affected, full of vanity:
Strangely ill natur'd, peevish and unkind,
Unconstant, false, to jealousy inclin'd:
His temper could not have so great a power,
'Tis mutable, and changes every hour:
Those vigorous years that women so adore
Are past in him: he's twice my age and more;
And yet I love this false, this worthless man,
With all the passion that a woman can;
Doat on his imperfections, though I spy
Nothing to love; I love, and know not why.
Since 'tis decreed in the dark book of Fate,
That I should love, and he should be ingrate.

She Walks in Beauty

by George Gordon Byron

She walks in beauty, like the night
Of cloudless climes and starry skies;
And all that's best of dark and bright
Meet in her aspect and her eyes:
Thus mellowed to that tender light
Which heaven to gaudy day denies.

One shade the more, one ray the less,
Had half impaired the nameless grace
Which waves in every raven tress,
Or softly lightens o'er her face;
Where thoughts serenely sweet express,
How pure, how dear their dwelling-place.

And on that cheek, and o'er that brow,
So soft, so calm, yet eloquent,
The smiles that win, the tints that glow,
But tell of days in goodness spent,
A mind at peace with all below,
A heart whose love is innocent!

When We Two Parted

by George Gordon Byron

When we two parted
　　In silence and tears,
Half broken-hearted
　　To sever for years,
Pale grew thy cheek and cold,
　　Colder thy kiss;
Truly that hour foretold
　　Sorrow to this.

The dew of the morning
　　Sunk chill on my brow—
It felt like the warning
　　Of what I feel now.
Thy vows are all broken,
　　And light is thy fame:

I hear thy name spoken,
    And share in its shame.

They name thee before me,
    A knell to mine ear;
A shudder comes o'er me—
    Why wert thou so dear?
They know not I knew thee,
    Who knew thee too well:
Long, long shall I rue thee,
    Too deeply to tell.

In secret we met—
    In silence I grieve,
That thy heart could forget,
    Thy spirit deceive.
If I should meet thee
    After long years,
How should I greet thee?
With silence and tears.

From Don Juan

by George Gordon Byron

CLXXXVI

A long, long kiss, a kiss of youth, and love,
    And beauty, all concentrating like rays
Into one focus, kindled from above;
    Such kisses as belong to early days,
Where heart, and soul, and sense, in concert
      move,
    And the blood's lava, and the pulse a blaze,
Each kiss a heart-quake,—for a kiss's strength,
I think it must be reckoned by its length.

CLXXXVII

By length I mean duration; theirs endured
    Heaven knows how long—no doubt they
      never reckoned;

And if they had, they could not have secured
    The sum of their sensations to a second:
They had not spoken, but they felt allured,
    As if their souls and lips each other beckoned,
Which, being joined, like swarming bees they clung—
Their hearts the flowers from whence the honey
    sprung.

To Little or No Purpose

by George Etherege

To little or no purpose have I spent all my days
In ranging the Park, th' Exchange, and the Plays,
Yet ne'er in my Rambles till now did I prove
So happy, to meet with the man I could love.
  But, O how I'm pleased when I think of the man
  That I find I must love, let me do what I can!

How long I shall love him, I can no more tell,
Than had I a Fever, when I should be well:
My Passion shall kill me before I will show it,
And yet I would give all the world he did know it:
  But, O how I sigh, when I think, should he woo me,
  That I cannot deny what I know will undo me!

Love

by George Herbert

Love bade me welcome; yet my soul drew back,
    Guilty of dust and sin.
But quick-eyed Love, observing me grow slack
    From my first entrance in,
Drew nearer to me, sweetly questioning
    If I lack'd anything.

'A guest,' I answer'd, 'worthy to be here:'
    Love said, 'You shall be he.'
'I, the unkind, ungrateful? Ah, my dear,
    I cannot look on Thee.'
Love took my hand and smiling did reply,
    'Who made the eyes but I?'

'Truth, Lord; but I have marr'd them: let my shame
    Go where it doth deserve.'
'And know you not,' says Love, 'Who bore the blame?'
    'My dear, then I will serve.'
'You must sit down,' says Love, 'and taste my meat.'
    So I did sit and eat.

Song

by George Lyttelton

When Delia on the plain appears,
Awed by a thousand tender fears,
I would approach, but dare not move;—
Tell me, my heart, if this be love.

Whene'er she speaks, my ravished ear
No other voice than hers can hear;
No other wit but hers approve;—
Tell me, my heart, if this be love.

If she some other swain commend,
Though I was once his fondest friend,
His instant enemy I prove;—
Tell me, my heart, if this be love.

When she is absent, I no more
Delight in all that pleased before,
The clearest spring, the shadiest grove;—
Tell me, my heart, if this be love.

When fond of power, of beauty vain,
Her nets she spread for every swain,
I strove to hate, but vainly strove;—
Tell me, my heart, if this be love.

Love in the Valley

by George Meredith

Under yonder beech-tree standing on the green
    sward,
Couched with her arms behind her little head,
Her knees folded up, and her tresses on her
    bosom,
Lies my young love sleeping in the shade.
Had I the heart to slide one arm beneath her!
Press her dreaming lips as her waist I folded slow,
Waking on the instant she could not but
    embrace me—
Ah! would she hold me, and never let me go?

Shy as the squirrel, and wayward as the swallow;
Swift as the swallow when, athwart the western
    flood,

Circleting the surface, he meets his mirrored winglets,
Is that dear one in her maiden bud.
Shy as the squirrel whose nest is in the pine-tops;
Gentle—ah! that she were jealous—as the dove!
Full of all the wildness of the woodland creatures,
Happy in herself is the maiden that I love!

What can have taught her distrust of all I tell her?
Can she truly doubt me when looking on my brows?
Nature never teaches distrust of tender love-tales;
What can have taught her distrust of all my vows?
No, she does not doubt me! on a dewy eve-tide,
Whispering together beneath the listening moon,
I prayed till her cheek flushed, implored till she
    faltered—
Fluttered to my bosom—ah! to fly away so soon!

When her mother tends her before the laughing
    mirror,
Tying up her laces, looping up her hair,
Often she thinks—were this wild thing wedded,
I should have more love, and much less care.
When her mother tends her before the bashful
    mirror,
Loosening her laces, combing down her curls,
Often she thinks—were this wild thing wedded,
I should lose but one for so many boys and girls.

Clambering roses peep into her chamber,
Jasmine and woodbine breathe sweet, sweet;
White-necked swallows, twittering of summer,
Fill her with balm and nested peace from head to
    feet.
Ah! will the rose-bough see her lying lonely,
When the petals fall and fierce bloom is on the leaves?
Will the autumn garners see her still ungathered,
When the fickle swallows forsake the weeping eaves?

Comes a sudden question—should a strange hand
    pluck her!
Oh! what an anguish smites me at the thought!
Should some idle lordling bribe her mind with jewels!
Can such beauty ever thus be bought?
Sometimes the huntsmen, prancing down the valley,
Eye the village lasses, full of sprightly mirth;
They see, as I see, mine is the fairest!
Would she were older and could read my worth!

Are there not sweet maidens, if she still deny me?
Show the bridal heavens but one bright star?
Wherefore thus then do I chase a shadow,
Clattering one note like a brown eve-jar?
So I rhyme and reason till she darts before me—
Through the milky meadows from flower to flower
    she flies,

Sunning her sweet palms to shade her dazzled eyelids
From the golden love that looks too eager in her eyes.

When at dawn she wakens, and her fair face gazes
Out on the weather through the window panes,
Beauteous she looks! like a white water-lily
Bursting out of bud on the rippled river plains.
When from bed she rises, clothed from neck to ankle
In her long night gown, sweet as boughs of May,
Beauteous she looks! like a tall garden lily,
Pure from the night and perfect for the day!

Happy, happy time, when the gray star twinkles
Over the fields all fresh with bloomy dew;
When the cold-cheeked dawn grows ruddy up the
    twilight,
And the gold sun wakes and weds her in the blue.
Then when my darling tempts the early breezes,
She the only star that dies not with the dark!
Powerless to speak all the ardor of my passion,
I catch her little hand as we listen to the lark.

Shall the birds in vain then valentine their
    sweethearts?
Season after season tell a fruitless tale?
Will not the virgin listen to their voices?
Take the honeyed meaning, wear the bridal veil?

Fears she frosts of winter, fears she the bare
    branches?
Waits she the garlands of spring for her dower?
Is she a nightingale that will not be nested
Till the April woodland has built her bridal bower?

Then come, merry April, with all thy birds and
    beauties!
With thy crescent brows and thy flowery, showery
    glee;
With thy budding leafage and fresh green pastures;
And may thy lustrous crescent grow a honeymoon
    for me!
Come, merry month of the cuckoo and the violet!
Come, weeping loveliness in all thy blue delight!
Lo! the nest is ready, let me not languish longer!
Bring her to my arms on the first May night.

Sonnet Upon a Stolen Kiss

by George Wither

Now gentle sleep hath closèd up those eyes
Which, waking, kept my boldest thoughts in
    awe;
And free access unto that sweet lip lies,
From whence I long the rosy breath to draw.
Methinks no wrong it were, if I should steal
From those two melting rubies one poor kiss;
None sees the theft that would the theft reveal,
Nor rob I her of aught what she can miss:
Nay, should I twenty kisses take away,
There would be little sign I would do so;
Why then should I this robbery delay?
O, she may awake, and therewith angry grow!
Well, if she do, I 'll back restore that one,
And twenty hundred thousand more for loan.

The Lover's Fate

by James Thomson

Hard is the fate of him who loves,
Yet dares not tell his trembling pain,
But to the sympathetic groves,
But to the lonely listening plain.

Oh! when she blesses next your shade,
Oh! when her footsteps next are seen
In flowery tracts along the mead,
In fresher mazes o'er the green;

Ye gentle spirits of the vale,
To whom the tears of love are dear,
From dying lilies waft a gale,
And sigh my sorrows in her ear.

Oh! tell her what she cannot blame,
Though fear my tongue must ever bind;
Oh, tell her, that my virtuous flame
Is, as her spotless soul, refined.

Not her own guardian-angel eyes
With chaster tenderness his care,
Not purer her own wishes rise,
Not holier her own sighs in prayer.

But if, at first, her virgin fear
Should start at love's suspected name,
With that of friendship soothe her ear—
True love and friendship are the same.

The Good Morrow

by John Donne

I wonder by my troth, what thou, and I
Did, till we lov'd? were we not wean'd till then?
But suck'd on countrey pleasures, childishly?
Or snorted we in the seaven sleepers den?
T'was so; But this, all pleasures fancies bee.
If ever any beauty I did see,
Which I desir'd, and got, t'was but a dreame of
        thee.

And now good morrow to our waking soules,
Which watch not one another out of feare;
For love, all love of other sights controules,
And makes one little roome, an every where.
Let sea-discoverers to new worlds have gone,
Let Maps to other, worlds on worlds have showne,

Let us possesse one world, each hath one, and
   is one.

My face in thine eye, thine in mine appeares,
And true plaine hearts doe in the faces rest,
Where can we finde two better hemispheares
Without sharpe North, without declining West?
What ever dyes, was not mixt equally;
If our two loves be one, or, thou and I
Love so alike, that none doe slacken, none can die.

The Sunne Rising

by John Donne

Busie old foole, unruly Sunne,
Why dost thou thus,
Through windowes, and through curtaines call
on us?
Must to thy motions lovers seasons run?
Sawcy pedantique wretch, goe chide
Late schoole boyes, and sowre prentices,
Goe tell Court-huntsmen, that the King
will ride,
Call countrey ants to harvest offices;
Love, all alike, no season knowes, nor clyme,
Nor houres, dayes, moneths, which are the rags
of time.

          Thy beames, so reverend, and strong
          Why shouldst thou thinke?
I could eclipse and cloud them with a winke,
But that I would not lose her sight so long:
          If her eyes have not blinded thine,
          Looke, and to morrow late, tell mee,
       Whether both the'India's of spice and Myne
      Be where thou leftst them, or lie here with
          mee.
Aske for those Kings whom thou saw'st yesterday,
And thou shalt heare, All here in one bed lay.
          She'is all States, and all Princes, I,
          Nothing else is.
Princes doe but play us; compar'd to this,
All honor's mimique; All wealth alchimie.
          Thou sunne art halfe as happy'as wee,
          In that the world's contracted thus;
       Thine age askes ease, and since thy duties bee
      To warme the world, that's done in warming us.
Shine here to us, and thou art every where;
This bed thy center is, these walls, thy spheare.

To His Mistress Going to Bed

by John Donne

Come, madam, come, all rest my powers defy,
Until I labor, I in labor lie.
The foe oft-times having the foe in sight,
Is tired with standing though he never fight.
Off with that girdle, like heaven's zone glistering,
But a far fairer world encompassing.
Unpin that spangled breastplate which you wear,
That th' eyes of busy fools may be stopped there.
Unlace yourself, for that harmonious chime
Tells me from you that now it is bed time.
Off with that happy busk, which I envy,
That still can be, and still can stand so nigh.
Your gown, going off, such beauteous state
    reveals, as when from flowry meads th'
    hill's shadow steals.

Off with that wiry coronet and show
The hairy diadem which on you doth grow:
Now off with those shoes, and then safely tread
In this love's hallowed temple, this soft bed.
In such white robes, heaven's angels used to be
Received by men; thou, Angel, bring'st with thee
A heaven like Mahomet's Paradise; and though
Ill spirits walk in white, we easily know
By this these angels from an evil sprite:
Those set our hairs on end, but these our flesh
    upright.
    License my roving hands, and let them go
Before, behind, between, above, below.
O my America! my new-found-land,
My kingdom, safeliest when with one man manned,
My mine of precious stones, my empery,
How blest am I in this discovering thee!
To enter in these bonds is to be free;
Then where my hand is set, my seal shall be.
    Full nakedness! All joys are due to thee,
As souls unbodied, bodies unclothed must be
To taste whole joys. Gems which you women use
Are like Atlanta's balls, cast in men's views,
That when a fool's eye lighteth on a gem,
His earthly soul may covet theirs, not them.
Like pictures, or like books' gay coverings made
For lay-men, are all women thus arrayed;

Themselves are mystic books, which only we
(Whom their imputed grace will dignify)
Must see revealed. Then, since that I may know,
As liberally as to a midwife, show
Thyself: cast all, yea, this white linen hence,
There is no penance due to innocence.

    To teach thee, I am naked first; why than,
what needst thou have more covering than a man?

Blue Eyes

by John Keats

Answer to a Sonnet Ending Thus—

"Dark eyes are dearer far
Than those that made the hyacinthine bell."
    By T. H. Reynolds.

Blue! 'T is the life of heaven,—the domain
    Of Cynthia,—the wide palace of the sun,—
The tent of Hesperus, and all his train,—
    The bosom of clouds, gold, gray, and dun.
Blue! 'T is the life of waters—ocean
    And all its vassal streams: pools numberless
May rage, and foam, and fret, but never can
    Subside, if not to dark-blue nativeness.
Blue! Gentle cousin of the forest-green,

Married to green in all the sweetest flowers—
Forget-me-not,—the blue-bell,—and, that queen
    Of secrecy, the violet: what strange powers
Hast thou, as a mere shadow! But how great,
    When in an Eye thou art alive with fate!

Bright Star

by John Keats

Bright star, would I were steadfast as thou art—
    Not in lone splendour hung aloft the night
And watching, with eternal lids apart,
    Like nature's patient, sleepless Eremite,
The moving waters at their priestlike task
    Of pure ablution round earth's human shores,
Or gazing on the new soft-fallen mask
    Of snow upon the mountains and the
        moors—
No—yet still stedfast, still unchangeable,
    Pillowed upon my fair love's ripening breast,
To feel for ever its soft fall and swell,
    Awake for ever in a sweet unrest,
Still, still to hear her tender-taken breath,
And so live ever—or else swoon to death.

La Belle Dame Sans Merci

by John Keats

O what can ail thee, knight-at-arms,
  Alone and palely loitering?
The sedge has wither'd from the lake,
  And no birds sing.

O what can ail thee, knight-at-arms!
  So haggard and so woe-begone?
The squirrel's granary is full,
  And the harvest's done.

I see a lily on thy brow
  With anguish moist and fever dew,
And on thy cheeks a fading rose
  Fast withereth too.

I met a lady in the meads,
    Full beautiful—a faery's child,
Her hair was long, her foot was light,
    And her eyes were wild.

I made a garland for her head,
    And bracelets too, and fragrant zone;
She look'd at me as she did love,
    And made sweet moan.

I set her on my pacing steed,
    And nothing else saw all day long,
For sidelong would she bend, and sing
    A faery's song.

She found me roots of relish sweet,
    And honey wild, and manna dew,
And sure in language strange she said—
    "I love thee true."

She took me to her elfin grot,
    And there she wept, and sigh'd fill sore,
And there I shut her wild wild eyes
    With kisses four.

And there she lulled me asleep,
    And there I dream'd—Ah! woe betide!

The latest dream I ever dream'd
    On the cold hill's side.

I saw pale kings and princes too,
    Pale warriors, death-pale were they all;
They cried—'La Belle Dame sans Merci
    Hath thee in thrall!'

I saw their starved lips in the gloam,
    With horrid warning gaped wide,
And I awoke and found me here,
    On the cold hill's side.

And this is why I sojourn here,
    Alone and palely loitering,
Though the sedge is wither'd from the lake,
    And no birds sing.

To Fanny

by John Keats

I cry your mercy—pity—love—ay, love!
    Merciful love that tantalizes not,
One-thoughted, never-wandering, guileless
    love,
        Unmasked, and being seen—without a
            blot!
O! let me have thee whole,—all—all—be mine!
    That shape, that fairness, that sweet minor
        zest
Of love, your kiss,—those hands, those eyes
    divine,
        That warm, white, lucent, million-pleasured
           breast,—
Yourself—your soul—in pity give me all,
    Withhold no atom's atom or I die,

Or living on perhaps, your wretched thrall,
    Forget, in the mist of idle misery,
Life's purposes,—the palate of my mind,
Losing its gust, and my ambition blind!

Constancy

by John Suckling

Out upon it. I have loved
    Three whole days together;
And am like to love three more,
    If it prove fair weather.

Time shall moult away his wings,
    Ere he shall discover
In the whole wide world again
    Such a constant lover.

But the spite on 't is, no praise
    Is due at all to me;
Love with me had made no stays,
    Had it any been but she.

Had it any been but she,
  And that very face,
There had been at least ere this
  A dozen in her place.

Endymion
(an extract)

by John Keats

A thing of beauty is a joy forever:
Its loveliness increases; it will never
Pass into nothingness; but still will keep
A bower quiet for us, and a sleep
Full of sweet dreams, and health, and quiet
    breathing.
Therefore, on every morrow, are we wreathing
A flowery band to bind us to the earth,
Spite of despondence, of the inhuman dearth
Of noble natures, of the gloomy days,
Of all the unhealthy and o'er-darkened ways
Made for our searching: yes, in spite of all,
Some shape of beauty moves away the pall
From our dark spirits. Such the sun, the moon,
Trees old and young, sprouting a shady boon

For simple sheep; and such are daffodils
With the green world they live in; and clear rills
That for themselves a cooling covert make
'Gainst the hot season; the mid-forest brake,
Rich with a sprinkling of fair musk-rose blooms:
And such too is the grandeur of the dooms
We have imagined for the mighty dead;
All lovely tales that we have heard or read:
An endless fountain of immortal drink,
Pouring unto us from the heaven's brink.

Fly to the Desert, Fly with Me

by Thomas Moore

"Fly to the desert, fly with me,
Our Arab tents are rude for thee;
But oh! the choice what heart can doubt
Of tents with love or thrones without?

"Our rocks are rough, but smiling there
The acacia waves her yellow hair,
Lonely and sweet, nor loved the less
For flowering in the wilderness.

"Our sands are bare, but down their slope
The silvery-footed antelope
As gracefully and gayly springs
As o'er the marble courts of kings.

"Then come,—thy Arab maid will be
The loved and lone acacia-tree,
The antelope, whose feet shall bless
With their light sound thy loneliness.

"Oh! there are looks and tones that dart
An instant sunshine through the heart,
As if the soul that minute caught
Some treasure it through life had sought;

"As if the very lips and eyes
Predestined to have all our sighs,
And never be forgot again,
Sparkled and spoke before as then!

"So came thy every glance and tone,
When first on me they breathed and shone;
New, as if brought from other spheres,
Yet welcome as if loved for years!

"Then fly with me, if thou hast known
No other flame, nor falsely thrown
A gem away, that thou hadst sworn
Should ever in thy heart be worn.

"Come, if the love thou hast for me
Is pure and fresh as mine for thee,—

Fresh as the fountain underground,
When first 't is by the lapwing found.

"But if for me thou dost forsake
Some other maid, and rudely break
Her worshipped image from its base,
To give to me the ruined place;

"Then, fare thee well!—I 'd rather make
My bower upon some icy lake
When thawing suns begin to shine,
Than trust to love so false as thine!"

There was a pathos in this lay,
    That even without enchantment's art
Would instantly have found its way
    Deep into Selim's burning heart;
But breathing, as it did, a tone
To earthly lutes and lips unknown;
With every chord fresh from the touch
Of music's spirit, 't was too much!
Starting, he dashed away the cup,—
    Which, all the time of this sweet air,
His hand had held, untasted, up,
    As if 't were fixed by magic there,
And naming her, so long unnamed,
So long unseen, wildly exclaimed,

"O Nourmahal! O Nourmahal!
    Hadst thou but sung this witching strain,
I could forget—forgive thee all,
    And never leave those eyes again."

The mask is off,—the charm is wrought,—
And Selim to his heart has caught,
In blushes, more than ever bright,
His Nourmahal, his Harem's Light!
And well do vanished frowns enhance
The charm of every brightened glance;
And dearer seems each dawning smile
For having lost its light awhile;
And, happier now for all her sighs,
    As on his arm her head reposes,
She whispers him, with laughing eyes,
    "Remember, love, the Feast of Roses!"

Since There's No Help

by Michael Drayton

Since there's no help, come let us kiss and
   part,—
Nay I have done, you get no more of me;
And I am glad, yea glad with all my heart,
That thus so cleanly I myself can free;
Shake hands for ever, cancel all our vows,
And when we meet at any time again,
Be it not seen in either of our brows
That we one jot of former love retain.
Now at the last gasp of love's latest breath,
When his pulse failing, passion speechless lies,
When faith is kneeling by his bed of death,
And innocence is closing up his eyes,
—Now if thou would'st, when all have given
   him over,
From death to life thou might'st him yet recover!

Her Voice

by Oscar Wilde

The wild bee reels from bough to bough
　　With his furry coat and his gauzy wing.
Now in a lily-cup, and now
　　Setting a jacinth bell a-swing,
　　　　In his wandering;
Sit closer love: it was here I trow
　　　　I made that vow,

Swore that two lives should be like one
　　As long as the sea-gull loved the sea,
As long as the sunflower sought the sun,—
　　It shall be, I said, for eternity
　　　　'Twixt you and me!
Dear friend, those times are over and done,
　　　　Love's web is spun.

Look upward where the poplar trees
    Sway and sway in the summer air,
Here in the valley never a breeze
    Scatters the thistledown, but there
      Great winds blow fair
From the mighty murmuring mystical seas,
      And the wave-lashed leas.

Look upward where the white gull screams,
    What does it see that we do not see?
Is that a star? or the lamp that gleams
    On some outward voyaging argosy,—
      Ah! can it be
We have lived our lives in a land of dreams!
      How sad it seems.

Sweet, there is nothing left to say
    But this, that love is never lost,
Keen winter stabs the breasts of May
    Whose crimson roses burst his frost,
      Ships tempest-tossed
Will find a harbour in some bay,
      And so we may.

And there is nothing left to do
    But to kiss once again, and part,
Nay, there is nothing we should rue,

I have my beauty,—you your Art,
    Nay, do not start,
One world was not enough for two
    Like me and you.

The Ballad of Reading Gaol
(an extract)

by Oscar Wilde

Yet each man kills the thing he loves,
    By each let this be heard,
    Some do it with a bitter look,
    Some with a flattering word,
    The coward does it with a kiss,
    The brave man with a sword!

Some kill their love when they are young,
    And some when they are old;
    Some strangle with the hands of Lust,
    Some with the hands of Gold:
    The kindest use a knife, because
    The dead so soon grow cold.
    Some love too little, some too long,

Some sell, and others buy;
Some do the deed with many tears,
And some without a sigh:
For each man kills the thing he loves,
Yet each man does not die.

Lines to an Indian Air

by Percy Bysshe Shelley

I arise from dreams of thee
    In the first sweet sleep of night,
When the winds are breathing low,
    And the stars are shining bright.
I arise from dreams of thee,
    And a spirit in my feet
Has led me—who knows how?—
    To thy chamber-window, sweet!

The wandering airs they faint
    On the dark, the silent stream,—
The champak odors fail
    Like sweet thoughts in a dream;
The nightingale's complaint,
    It dies upon her heart,

As I must die on thine,
    O, belovèd as thou art!

O, lift me from the grass!
    I die, I faint, I fail!
Let thy love in kisses rain
    On my lips and eyelids pale.
My cheek is cold and white, alas!
    My heart beats loud and fast:
O, press it close to thine again,
Where it will break at last!

Love's Philosophy

by Percy Bysshe Shelley

The fountains mingle with the river,
And the rivers with the ocean,
The winds of heaven mix for ever
With a sweet emotion;
Nothing in the world is single;
All things by a law divine
In one another's being mingle
Why not I with thine?

See, the mountains kiss high heaven
And the waves clasp one another;
No sister-flower would be forgiven
If it disdained its brother:
And the sunlight clasps the earth

And the moonbeams kiss the sea,
What is all this sweet work worth,
If thou kiss not me?

Music When
Soft Voices Die

by Percy Bysshe Shelley

Music, when soft voices die,
Vibrates in the memory—
Odours, when sweet violets sicken,
Live within the sense they quicken.

Rose leaves, when the rose is dead,
Are heaped for the belovèd's bed;
And so thy thoughts, when thou art gone,
Love itself shall slumber on.

My True-Love Hath My Heart

A Song from *Arcadia*
by Philip Sidney

My true-love hath my heart and I have his,
By just exchange one for the other given:
I hold his dear, and mine he cannot miss;
There never was a bargain better driven.
His heart in me keeps me and him in one;
My heart in him his thoughts and senses guides:
He loves my heart, for once it was his own;
I cherish his because in me it bides.
His heart his wound received from my sight;
My heart was wounded with his wounded heart;
For as from me on him his hurt did light,
So still, methought, in me his hurt did smart:
Both equal hurt, in this change sought our bliss,
My true love hath my heart and I have his.

If Thou Wert by My Side, My Love

by Reginald Heber

If thou wert by my side, my love!
   How fast would evening fail
In green Bengala's palmy grove,
   Listening the nightingale!

If thou, my love, wert by my side,
   My babies at my knee,
How gayly would our pinnace glide
   O'er Gunga's mimic sea!

I miss thee at the dawning gray,
   When, on our deck reclined,
In careless ease my limbs I lay
   And woo the cooler wind.

I miss thee when by Gunga's stream
 My twilight steps I guide,
But most beneath the lamp's pale beam
 I miss thee from my side.

I spread my books, my pencil try,
 The lingering noon to cheer,
But miss thy kind, approving eye,
 Thy meek, attentive ear.

But when at morn and eve the star
 Beholds me on my knee,
I feel, though thou art distant far,
 Thy prayers ascend for me.

Then on! then on! where duty leads,
 My course be onward still,
O'er broad Hindostan's sultry meads,
 O'er bleak Almorah's hill.

That course nor Delhi's kingly gates,
 Nor mild Malwah detain;
For sweet the bliss us both awaits
 By yonder western main.

Thy towers, Bombay, gleam bright, they say,
　　Across the dark blue sea;
But never were hearts so light and gay
　　As then shall meet in thee!

Not Until Next Time

by Richard Doddridge Blackmore

"I dreamed that we were lovers still,
    As tender as we used to be
When I brought you the daffodil,
    And you looked up and smiled at me."

"True sweethearts were we then, indeed,
    When youth was budding into bloom;
And now the flowers are gone to seed,
    And breezes have left no perfume."

"Because you ever, ever will
    Take such a crooked view of things,
Distorting this and that, until
    Confusion ends in cavillings."

"Because you never, never will
     Perceive the force of what I say;
As if I always reasoned ill—
     Enough to take one's breath away!"

"But what if riper love replace
     The vision that enchanted me,
When all you did was perfect grace,
     And all you said was melody?"

"And what if loyal heart renew
     The image never quite foregone,
Combining, as of yore, in you
     A Samson and a Solomon?"

"Then to the breezes will I toss
     The straws we split with temper's loss;
Then seal upon your lips anew
     The peace that gentle hearts ensue."

"Oh, welcome then, ye playful ways,
     And sunshine of the early days;
And banish to the clouds above
     Dull reason, that bedarkens love!"

Now

by Robert Browning

Out of your whole life give but one moment!
All of your life that has gone before,
All to come after it,—so you ignore,
So you make perfect the present,—condense,
In a rapture of rage, for perfection's endowment,
Thought and feeling and soul and sense—
Merged in a moment which gives me at last
You around me for once, you beneath me,
    above me—
Me—sure that despite of time future, time
    past,—
This tick of our life-time's one moment you
    love me!
How long such suspension may linger? Ah,
    Sweet—

The moment eternal—just that and no more—
When ecstasy's utmost we clutch at the core
While cheeks burn, arms open, eyes shut and lips
    meet!

Life in a Love

by Robert Browning

Escape me?
Never—
Beloved!
While I am I, and you are you,
So long as the world contains us both,
Me the loving and you the loth,
While the one eludes, must the other pursue.
My life is a fault at last, I fear:
It seems too much like a fate, indeed!
Though I do my best I shall scarce succeed.
But what if I fail of my purpose here?
It is but to keep the nerves at strain,
To dry one's eyes and laugh at a fall,
And, baffled, get up and begin again,—
So the chase takes up one's life, that's all.

While, look but once from your farthest bound
At me so deep in the dust and dark,
No sooner the old hope goes to ground
Than a new one, straight to the self-same mark,
I shape me—
Ever
Removed!

Porphyria's Lover

by Robert Browning

The rain set early in tonight,
    The sullen wind was soon awake,
It tore the elm-tops down for spite,
    And did its worst to vex the lake:
    I listened with heart fit to break.
When glided in Porphyria; straight
    She shut the cold out and the storm,
And kneeled and made the cheerless grate
    Blaze up, and all the cottage warm;
    Which done, she rose, and from her form
Withdrew the dripping cloak and shawl,
    And laid her soiled gloves by, untied
Her hat and let the damp hair fall,
    And, last, she sat down by my side
    And called me. When no voice replied,

She put my arm about her waist,
    And made her smooth white shoulder bare,
And all her yellow hair displaced,
    And, stooping, made my cheek lie there,
    And spread, o'er all, her yellow hair,
Murmuring how she loved me—she
    Too weak, for all her heart's endeavour,
To set its struggling passion free
    From pride, and vainer ties dissever,
    And give herself to me for ever.
But passion sometimes would prevail,
    Nor could to-night's gay feast restrain
A sudden thought of one so pale
    For love of her, and all in vain:
    So, she was come through wind and rain.
Be sure I looked up at her eyes
    Happy and proud; at last I knew
Porphyria worshipped me; surprise
    Made my heart swell, and still it grew
    While I debated what to do.
That moment she was mine, mine, fair,
    Perfectly pure and good: I found
A thing to do, and all her hair
    In one long yellow string I wound
    Three times her little throat around,
And strangled her. No pain felt she;
    I am quite sure she felt no pain.

As a shut bud that holds a bee,
    I warily oped her lids: again
    Laughed the blue eyes without a stain.
And I untightened next the tress
    About her neck; her cheek once more
Blushed bright beneath my burning kiss:
    I propped her head up as before,
    Only, this time my shoulder bore
Her head, which droops upon it still:
    The smiling rosy little head,
So glad it has its utmost will,
    That all it scorned at once is fled,
    And I, its love, am gained instead!
Porphyria's love: she guessed not how
    Her darling one wish would be heard.
And thus we sit together now,
    And all night long we have not stirred,
    And yet God has not said a word!

In Three Days

by Robert Browning

So, I shall see her in three days
And just one night, but nights are short,
Then two long hours, and that is morn.
See how I come, unchanged, unworn!
Feel, where my life broke off from thine,
How fresh the splinters keep and fine—
Only a touch and we combine!

Too long, this time of year, the days!
But nights, at least the nights are short.
As night shows where her one moon is,
A hand's-breadth of pure light and bliss,
So life's night gives my lady birth
And my eyes hold her!
What is worth
The rest of heaven, the rest of earth?

O loaded curls, release your store
Of warmth and scent, as once before
The tingling hair did, lights and darks
Outbreaking into fairy sparks,
When under curl and curl I pried
After the warmth and scent inside,
Through lights and darks how manifold—
The dark inspired, the light controlled!
As early Art embrowns the gold.

What great fear, should one say, "Three days
That change the world might change as well
Your fortune; and if joy delays,
Be happy that no worse befell!
"What small fear, if another says,
"Three days and one short night beside
May throw no shadow on your ways;
But years must teem with change untried,
With chance not easily defied,
With an end somewhere undescried.
"No fear!—or if a fear be born
This minute, it dies out in scorn.
Fear? I shall see her in three days
And one night, now the nights are short,
Then just two hours, and that is morn.

A Red, Red Rose

by Robert Burns

O my Luve's like a red, red rose
    That's newly sprung in June;
O my Luve's like the melodie
    That's sweetly played in tune.

As fair art thou my bonnie lass,
    So deep in luve am I;
And I will luve thee still, my dear,
    Till a' the seas gang dry.

Till a' the seas gang dry, my dear,
    And the rocks melt wi' the sun;
I will love thee still, my dear,
    While the sands o' life shall run.

And fare thee weel, my only Luve!
    And fare thee weel, awhile!
And I will come again, my Luve,
    Tho' it were ten thousand mile.

Let Not Woman E'er Complain

by Robert Burns

Let not woman e'er complain
    Of inconstancy in love;
Let not woman e'er complain
    Fickle man is apt to rove;
Look abroad through Nature's range,
Nature's mighty law is change;
Ladies, would it not be strange
    Man should then a monster prove?

Mark the winds, and mark the skies;
    Ocean's ebb and ocean's flow;
Sun and moon but set to rise,
    Round and round the seasons go.

Why then ask of silly man,
To oppose great Nature's plan?
We'll be constant while we can,—
    You can be no more, you know.

To the Virgins,
to Make Much of Time

by Robert Herrick

Gather ye rose-buds while ye may,
Old Time is still a-flying;
And this same flower that smiles today
Tomorrow will be dying.

The glorious lamp of heaven, the sun,
The higher he's a-getting,
The sooner will his race be run,
And nearer he's to setting.

That age is best which is the first,
When youth and blood are warmer;
But being spent, the worse, and worst
Times still succeed the former.

Then be not coy, but use your time,
And while ye may, go marry;
For having lost but once your prime,
You may forever tarry.

Love

by Samuel Taylor Coleridge

All thoughts, all passions, all delights,
Whatever stirs this mortal frame,
All are but ministers of Love,
And feed his sacred flame.

Oft in my waking dreams do I
Live o'er again that happy hour,
When midway on the mount I lay,
Beside the ruined tower.

The moonshine, stealing o'er the scene
Had blended with the lights of eve;
And she was there, my hope, my joy,
My own dear Genevieve!

She leant against the arméd man,
The statue of the arméd knight;
She stood and listened to my lay,
Amid the lingering light.

Few sorrows hath she of her own,
My hope! my joy! my Genevieve!
She loves me best, whene'er I sing
The songs that make her grieve.

I played a soft and doleful air,
I sang an old and moving story—
An old rude song, that suited well
That ruin wild and hoary.

She listened with a flitting blush,
With downcast eyes and modest grace;
For well she knew, I could not choose
But gaze upon her face.

I told her of the Knight that wore
Upon his shield a burning brand;
And that for ten long years he wooed
The Lady of the Land.

I told her how he pined: and ah!
The deep, the low, the pleading tone

With which I sang another's love,
Interpreted my own.

She listened with a flitting blush,
With downcast eyes, and modest grace;
And she forgave me, that I gazed
Too fondly on her face!

But when I told the cruel scorn
That crazed that bold and lovely Knight,
And that he crossed the mountain-woods,
Nor rested day nor night;

That sometimes from the savage den,
And sometimes from the darksome shade,
And sometimes starting up at once
In green and sunny glade,—

There came and looked him in the face
An angel beautiful and bright;
And that he knew it was a Fiend,
This miserable Knight!

And that unknowing what he did,
He leaped amid a murderous band,
And saved from outrage worse than death
The Lady of the Land!

And how she wept, and clasped his knees;
And how she tended him in vain—
And ever strove to expiate
The scorn that crazed his brain;—

And that she nursed him in a cave;
And how his madness went away,
When on the yellow forest-leaves
A dying man he lay;—
His dying words—but when I reached
That tenderest strain of all the ditty,
My faultering voice and pausing harp
Disturbed her soul with pity!

All impulses of soul and sense
Had thrilled my guileless Genevieve;
The music and the doleful tale,
The rich and balmy eve;

And hopes, and fears that kindle hope,
An undistinguishable throng,
And gentle wishes long subdued,
Subdued and cherished long!

She wept with pity and delight,
She blushed with love, and virgin-shame;

And like the murmur of a dream,
I heard her breathe my name.

Her bosom heaved—she stepped aside,
As conscious of my look she stepped—
Then suddenly, with timorous eye
She fled to me and wept.

She half enclosed me with her arms,
She pressed me with a meek embrace;
And bending back her head, looked up,
And gazed upon my face.

'Twas partly love, and partly fear,
And partly 'twas a bashful art,
That I might rather feel, than see,
The swelling of her heart.

I calmed her fears, and she was calm,
And told her love with virgin pride;
And so I won my Genevieve,
My bright and beauteous Bride.

New Love and Old

by Sara Teasdale

In my heart the old love
Struggled with the new,
It was ghostly waking
All night through.

Dear things, kind things
That my old love said,
Ranged themselves reproachfully
Round my bed.

But I could not heed them,
For I seemed to see
Dark eyes of my new love
Fixed on me.

Old love, old love,
How can I be true?
Shall I be faithless to myself
Or to you?

The Kiss

by Sara Teasdale

I hoped that he would love me,
    And he has kissed my mouth,
But I am like a stricken bird
    That cannot reach the south.

For though I know he loves me,
    To-night my heart is sad;
His kiss was not so wonderful
    As all the dreams I had.

The First Kiss

by Thomas Campbell

How delicious is the winning
Of a kiss at love's beginning,
When two mutual hearts are sighing
For the knot there's no untying!

Yet remember, midst your wooing,
Love has bliss, but love has ruing;
Other smiles may make you fickle,
Tears for other charms may trickle.

Love he comes, Love he tarries,
Just as fate or fancy carries,—
Longest stays when sorest chidden,
Laughs and flies when pressed and bidden.

Bind the sea to slumber stilly,
Bind its odor to the lily,
Bind the aspen ne'er to quiver,—
Then bind Love to last forever!

Love's a fire that needs renewal
Of fresh beauty for its fuel;
Love's wing moults when caged and captured,—
Only free he soars enraptured.

Can you keep the bee from ranging,
Or the ring-dove's neck from changing?
No! nor fettered Love from dying
In the knot there's no untying.

A Rapture
(an extract)

by Thomas Carew

I will enjoy thee now, my Celia, come,
And fly with me to Love's Elysium,
The Giant, Honour, that keeps cowards out,
Is but a masquer, and the servile rout
Of baser subjects only bend in vain
To the vast Idol; whilst the nobler train
Of valiant Lovers daily sail between
The huge Colossus' legs, and pass unseen
Unto the blissful shore. Be bold and wise,
And we shall enter: the grim Swiss denies
    Only to fools a passage, that not know
    He is but form, and only frights in show.

Let duller eyes that look from far, draw near,
And they shall scorn what they were wont to fear.
We shall see how the stalking Pageant goes
With borrow'd legs, a heavy load to those
That made and bear him: not, as we once thought,
The seed of Gods, but a weak model, wrought
     By greedy men, that seek to enclose the
          common,
     And within private arms impale free Woman.

     Come, then, and mounted on the wings of
          Love
We'll cut the fleeting air, and soar above
The Monster's head, and in the noblest seat
Of those blest shades quench and renew our heat.
There shall the Queens of Love and Innocence,
Beauty and Nature, banish all offence
From our close Ivy-twines: there I'll behold
Thy bared snow and thy unbraided gold;
There my enfranchised hand on every side
Shall o'er thy naked polish'd ivory slide.
No curtain there, though of transparent lawn,
Shall be before thy virgin-treasure drawn;
But the rich Mine, to the enquiring eye
Exposed, shall ready still for mintage lie:
And we will coin young Cupids. There a bed
Of roses and fresh myrtles shall be spread,

Under the cooler shade of Cypress groves;
Our pillows, of the down of Venus' doves;
Whereon our panting limbs we'll gently lay,
In the faint respites of our amorous play:
That so our slumbers may in dreams have leisure
To tell the nimble fancy our past pleasure,
 And so our souls—that cannot be embraced—
 Shall the embraces of our bodies taste.

A Broken Appointment

by Thomas Hardy

You did not come,
And marching Time drew on, and wore me
    numb.—
Yet less for loss of your dear presence there
Than that I thus found lacking in your make
That high compassion which can overbear
Reluctance for pure lovingkindness' sake
Grieved I, when, as the hope-hour stroked its
    sum,
    You did not come.

You love not me,
And love alone can lend you loyalty;
—I know and knew it. But, unto the store
Of human deeds divine in all but name,

Was it not worth a little hour or more
To add yet this: Once, you, a woman, came
To soothe a time-torn man; even though it be
    You love not me?

Song

by Thomas Middleton

Love is like a lamb, and love is like a lion;
Fly from love, he fights; fight, then does he fly on;
Love is all in fire, and yet is ever freezing;
Love is much in winning, yet is more in leezing;
Love is ever sick, and yet is never dying;
Love is ever true, and yet is ever lying;
Love does dote in liking, and is mad in loathing;
Love indeed is anything, and yet indeed is
    nothing.

A Joke Versified

by Thomas Moore

'Come, come,' said Tom's father, 'at your time
of life,
There's no longer excuse for thus playing
the rake.
It is time you should think, boy, of taking a wife.'
'Why, so it is, father. Whose wife shall I
take?'

They Flee from Me

by Thomas Wyatt

They flee from me that sometime did me seek
With naked foot, stalking in my chamber.
I have seen them gentle, tame, and meek,
That now are wild and do not remember
That sometime they put themself in danger
To take bread at my hand; and now they range,
Busily seeking with a continual change.

Thanked be fortune it hath been otherwise
Twenty times better; but once in special,
In thin array after a pleasant guise,
When her loose gown from her shoulders did
    fall,
And she me caught in her arms long and small;

Therewithall sweetly did me kiss
And softly said, "Dear heart, how like you this?"

It was no dream: I lay broad waking.
But all is turned thorough my gentleness
Into a strange fashion of forsaking;
And I have leave to go of her goodness,
And she also, to use newfangleness.
But since that I so kindly am served
I would fain know what she hath deserved.

Farewell Love

by Thomas Wyatt

Farewell love and all thy laws forever;
Thy baited hooks shall tangle me no more.
Senec and Plato call me from thy lore
To perfect wealth, my wit for to endeavour.
In blind error when I did persever,
Thy sharp repulse, that pricketh aye so sore,
Hath taught me to set in trifles no store
And scape forth, since liberty is lever.
Therefore farewell; go trouble younger hearts
And in me claim no more authority.
With idle youth go use thy property
And thereon spend thy many brittle darts,
For hitherto though I have lost all my time,
Me lusteth no lenger rotten boughs to climb.

A Glimpse

by Walt Whitman

A glimpse through an interstice caught,
Of a crowd of workmen and drivers in a
bar-room around the stove late of a
winter night, and I unremark'd seated
in a corner,
Of a youth who loves me and whom I
love, silently approaching and seating
himself near, that he may hold me by
the hand,
A long while amid the noises of coming
and going, of drinking and oath and
smutty jest,
There we two, content, happy in being
together, speaking little, perhaps not
a word.

To a Stranger

by Walt Whitman

Passing stranger! you do not know how longingly
    I look upon you,
You must be he I was seeking, or she I was
    seeking, (it comes to me, as of a dream,)
I have somewhere surely lived a life of joy with
    you,
All is recall'd as we flit by each other, fluid,
    affectionate, chaste, matured,
You grew up with me, were a boy with me, or
    a girl with me,
I ate with you, and slept with you—your body
    has become not yours only, nor left my
    body mine only,

You give me the pleasure of your eyes, face, flesh,
     as we pass—you take of my beard, breast,
     hands, in return,
I am not to speak to you—I am to think of you
     when I sit alone, or wake at night alone,
I am to wait—I do not doubt I am to meet you
     again,
I am to see to it that I do not lose you.

Farewell, False Love

by Walter Raleigh

Farewell, false love, the oracle of lies,
A mortal foe and enemy to rest,
An envious boy, from whom all cares arise,
A bastard vile, a beast with rage possessed,
A way of error, a temple full of treason,
In all effects contrary unto reason.

A poisoned serpent covered all with flowers,
Mother of sighs, and murderer of repose,
A sea of sorrows whence are drawn such
    showers
As moisture lend to every grief that grows;
A school of guile, a net of deep deceit,
A gilded hook that holds a poisoned bait.

A fortress foiled, which reason did defend,
A siren song, a fever of the mind,
A maze wherein affection finds no end,
A raging cloud that runs before the wind,
A substance like the shadow of the sun,
A goal of grief for which the wisest run.

A quenchless fire, a nurse of trembling fear,
A path that leads to peril and mishap,
A true retreat of sorrow and despair,
An idle boy that sleeps in pleasure's lap,
A deep mistrust of that which certain seems,
A hope of that which reason doubtful deems.

Sith then thy trains my younger years betrayed,
And for my faith ingratitude I find;
And sith repentance hath my wrongs bewrayed,
Whose course was ever contrary to kind:
False love, desire, and beauty frail, adieu!
Dead is the root whence all these fancies grew.

The Nymph's Reply to the Shepherd

by Walter Raleigh

If all the world and love were young,
And truth in every Shepherd's tongue,
These pretty pleasures might me move,
To live with thee, and be thy love.

Time drives the flocks from field to fold,
When Rivers rage and Rocks grow cold,
And *Philomel* becometh dumb,
The rest complains of cares to come.

The flowers do fade, and wanton fields,
To wayward winter reckoning yields,
A honey tongue, a heart of gall,
Is fancy's spring, but sorrow's fall.

Thy gowns, thy shoes, thy beds of Roses,
Thy cap, thy kirtle, and thy posies
Soon break, soon wither, soon forgotten:
In folly ripe, in reason rotten.

Thy belt of straw and Ivy buds,
The Coral clasps and amber studs,
All these in me no means can move
To come to thee and be thy love.

But could youth last, and love still breed,
Had joys no date, nor age no need,
Then these delights my mind might move
To live with thee, and be thy love.

As You Came from the Holy Land

by Walter Raleigh

As you came from the holy land
Of Walsingham,
Met you not with my true love
By the way as you came?

"How shall I know your true love,
That have met many one,
I went to the holy land,
That have come, that have gone?"

She is neither white, nor brown,
But as the heavens fair;
There is none hath a form so divine
In the earth, or the air.

"Such a one did I meet, good sir,
Such an angelic face,
Who like a queen, like a nymph, did appear
By her gait, by her grace."

She hath left me here all alone,
All alone, as unknown,
Who sometimes did me lead with herself,
And me loved as her own.

"What's the cause that she leaves you alone,
And a new way doth take,
Who loved you once as her own,
And her joy did you make?"

I have lov'd her all my youth;
But now old, as you see,
Love likes not the falling fruit
From the withered tree.

Know that Love is a careless child,
And forgets promise past;
He is blind, he is deaf when he list,
And in faith never fast.

His desire is a dureless content,
And a trustless joy:

He is won with a world of despair,
And is lost with a toy.

Of womenkind such indeed is the love,
Or the word love abus'd,
Under which many childish desires
And conceits are excus'd.

But true love is a durable fire,
In the mind ever burning,
Never sick, never old, never dead,
From itself never turning.

Love's Secret

by William Blake

Never seek to tell thy love,
   Love that never told can be;
For the gentle wind doth move
   Silently, invisibly.

I told my love, I told my love,
   I told her all my heart,
Trembling, cold, in ghastly fears.
   Ah! she did depart!

Soon after she was gone from me,
   A traveller came by,
Silently, invisibly:
   He took her with a sigh.

A Drinking Song

by W B Yeats

Wine comes in at the mouth
And love comes in at the eye;
That's all we shall know for truth
Before we grow old and die.
I lift the glass to my mouth,
I look at you, and I sigh.

A Poet to His Beloved

by W B Yeats

I bring you with reverent hands
The books of my numberless dreams;
White woman that passion has worn
As the tide wears the dove-gray sands,
And with heart more old than the horn
That is brimmed from the pale fire of time:
White woman with numberless dreams
I bring you my passionate rhyme.

Never Give All the Heart

by W B Yeats

Never give all the heart, for love
Will hardly seem worth thinking of
To passionate women if it seem
Certain, and they never dream
That it fades out from kiss to kiss;
For everything that's lovely is
But a brief, dreamy, kind delight.
O never give the heart outright,
For they, for all smooth lips can say,
Have given their hearts up to the play.
And who could play it well enough
If deaf and dumb and blind with love?
He that made this knows all the cost,
For he gave all his heart and lost.

When You Are Old

by W B Yeats

When you are old and grey and full of sleep,
And nodding by the fire, take down this book,
And slowly read, and dream of the soft look
Your eyes had once, and of their shadows deep;

How many loved your moments of glad grace,
And loved your beauty with love false or true,
But one man loved the pilgrim soul in you,
And loved the sorrows of your changing face;

And bending down beside the glowing bars,
Murmur, a little sadly, how Love fled
And paced upon the mountains overhead
And hid his face amid a crowd of stars.

The Worn Wedding Ring

by William Cox Bennett

Your wedding-ring wears thin, dear wife; ah,
　　summers not a few,
Since I put it on your finger first, have passed
　　o'er me and you;
And, love, what changes we have seen,—what
　　cares and pleasures, too,—
Since you became my own dear wife, when this
　　old ring was new!

O, blessings on that happy day, the happiest of
　　my life,
When, thanks to God, your low, sweet "Yes"
　　made you my loving wife!
Your heart will say the same, I know; that day's
　　as dear to you,—

That day that made me yours, dear wife, when this
old ring was new.

How well do I remember now your young sweet
face that day!
How fair you were, how dear you were, my tongue
could hardly say;
Nor how I doated on you; O, how proud I was of you!
But did I love you more than now, when this old
ring was new?

No—no! no fairer were you then than at this hour
to me;
And, dear as life to me this day, how could you
dearer be?
As sweet your face might be that day as now it is,
't is true;
But did I know your heart as well when this old
ring was new?

O partner of my gladness, wife, what care, what
grief is there
For me you would not bravely face, with me you
would not share?
O, what a weary want had every day, if wanting you,
Wanting the love that God made mine when this
old ring was new!

Years bring fresh links to bind us, wife,—young
    voices that are here;
Young faces round our fire that make their mother's
    yet more dear;
Young loving hearts your care each day makes yet
    more like to you,
More like the loving heart made mine when this
    old ring was new.

And blessed be God! all he has given are with us
    yet; around
Our table every precious life lent to us still is
    found.
Though cares we've known, with hopeful hearts
    the worst we've struggled through;
Blessed be his name for all his love since this old
    ring was new!

The past is dear, its sweetness still our memories
    treasure yet;
The griefs we've borne, together borne, we would
    not now forget.
Whatever, wife, the future brings, heart unto heart
    still true,
We'll share as we have shared all else since this old
    ring was new.

And if God spare us 'mongst our sons and daughters
    to grow old,
We know his goodness will not let your heart or
    mine grow cold.
Your aged eyes will see in mine all they've still
    shown to you,
And mine and yours all they have seen since this
    old ring was new!

And O, when death shall come at last to bid me to
    my rest,
May I die looking in those eyes, and resting on that
    breast;
O, may my parting gaze be blessed with the dear
    sight of you,
Of those fond eyes,—fond as they were when this
    old ring was new!

Summer Dawn

by William Morris

Pray but one prayer for me 'twixt thy closed
    lips,
    Think but one thought of me up in the stars.
The summer night waneth, the morning light
    slips
    Faint and gray 'twixt the leaves of the aspen,
        betwixt the cloud-bars,
That are patiently waiting there for the dawn:
    Patient and colourless, though Heaven's
        gold
Waits to float through them along with the sun.
Far out in the meadows, above the young corn,
    The heavy elms wait, and restless and cold
The uneasy wind rises; the roses are dun;

Through the long twilight they pray for the dawn
Round the lone house in the midst of the corn.
Speak but one word to me over the corn,
Over the tender, bow'd locks of the corn.

Let Me Not to the Marriage of True Minds

by William Shakespeare

Let me not to the marriage of true minds
    Admit impediments. Love is not love
    Which alters when it alteration finds,
    Or bends with the remover to remove.
    O no! it is an ever-fixed mark
    That looks on tempests and is never shaken;
    It is the star to every wand'ring bark,
    Whose worth's unknown, although his height
      be taken.
    Love's not Time's fool, though rosy lips and
      cheeks
    Within his bending sickle's compass come,
    Love alters not with his brief hours and
      weeks,

But bears it out even to the edge of doom:
If this be error and upon me proved,
I never writ, nor no man ever loved.

My Mistress' Eyes Are Nothing Like the Sun

by William Shakespeare

My mistress' eyes are nothing like the sun;
    Coral is far more red than her lips' red;
    If snow be white, why then her breasts are
        dun;
    If hairs be wires, black wires grow on her
        head.
I have seen roses damask'd, red and white,
But no such roses see I in her cheeks;
And in some perfumes is there more delight
Than in the breath that from my mistress
        reeks.
I love to hear her speak, yet well I know
That music hath a far more pleasing sound;
I grant I never saw a goddess go;

My mistress, when she walks, treads on the
      ground:
And yet, by heaven, I think my love as rare
As any she belied with false compare.

Shall I Compare Thee to a Summer's Day

by William Shakespeare

Shall I compare thee to a summer's day?
    Thou art more lovely and more temperate:
    Rough winds do shake the darling buds of
        May,
    And summer's lease hath all too short a date:
    Sometime too hot the eye of heaven shines,
    And often is his gold complexion dimm'd;
    And every fair from fair sometime declines,
    By chance, or nature's changing course,
        untrimm'd:
    But thy eternal summer shall not fade,
    Nor lose possession of that fair thou ow'st;
    Nor shall Death brag thou wander'st in his
        shade,

When in eternal lines to time thou grow'st:
So long as men can breathe, or eyes can see,
So long lives this, and this gives life to thee.

Venus and Adonis
(an extract)

by William Shakespeare

Had I no eyes but ears, my ears would love
That inward beauty and invisible;
Or were I deaf, thy outward parts would move
Each part in me that were but sensible:
Though neither eyes nor ears, to hear nor see,
Yet should I be in love by touching thee.

Say, that the sense of feeling were bereft me,
And that I could not see, nor hear, nor touch,
And nothing but the very smell were left me,
Yet would my love to thee be still as much;
For from the stillitory of thy face excelling
Comes breath perfumed that breedeth love by
    smelling.

She Was a Phantom
of Delight

by William Wordsworth

She was a phantom of delight
When first she gleamed upon my sight;
A lovely apparition, sent
To be a moment's ornament;
Her eyes as stars of twilight fair;
Like Twilight's, too, her dusky hair;
But all things else about her drawn
From May-time and the cheerful dawn;
A dancing shape, an image gay,
To haunt, to startle, and waylay.

I saw her upon nearer view,
A spirit, yet a woman too!
Her household motions light and free,
And steps of virgin-liberty;

A countenance in which did meet
Sweet records, promises as sweet;
A creature not too bright or good
For human nature's daily food,
For transient sorrows, simple wiles,
Praise, blame, love, kisses, tears, and smiles.

And now I see with eye serene
The very pulse of the machine;
A being breathing thoughtful breath,
A traveller between life and death:
The reason firm, the temperate will,
Endurance, foresight, strength, and skill;
A perfect woman, nobly planned
To warn, to comfort, and command;
And yet a spirit still, and bright
With something of an angel-light.

Index